For Rona Selby, for not being a chicken. J.W.

This paperback edition first published in 2015 Andersen Press Ltd.
First published in Great Britain in 2014 by Andersen Press Ltd., 20 Vauxhall Bridge Road, London SW1V 2SA.
Published in Australia by Random House Australia Pty., Level 3, 100 Pacific Highway, North Sydney, NSW 2060.
Text copyright © Jeanne Willis, 2014. Illustration copyright © Tony Ross, 2014.
The rights of Jeanne Willis and Tony Ross to be identified as the author and illustrator of this work
have been asserted by them in accordance with the Copyright, Designs and Patents Act, 1988.
All rights reserved. Printed and bound in Malaysia by Tien Wah Press.

10   9   8   7   6   5   4   3   2

British Library Cataloguing in Publication Data available.

ISBN 978 1 78344 161 7

CHICKEN CLICKING

JEANNE WILLIS   TONY ROSS

ANDERSEN PRESS

Once there was a little chick,
Chirpy, chirpy, cheep.

She hopped into the farmer's house
When he was fast asleep.

She crept into his study,
She tiptoed past the cat . . .

. . . And clicked on his computer
With the mouse upon the mat.

Cheepy, chirpy, cheepy – CLICK!
She had a little browse.

She bought a funny teapot – CLICK!
She bought a frilly blouse.

CLICK! She bought a motorbike.
CLICK! A hive of bees.

"Good heavens!" said the farmer.
"Did I really order these?"

The second night the chick came back
Cheepy, chirpy – CLICK!

She bought herself a diamond watch,
CLICK! Tock tick.

She bought a hundred handbags
And shoes from every site.

The farmer blamed his wife

Who said his software wasn't right.

The third night came and just the same
The chicken went online.

She ordered scooters for the sheep
And skates for all the swine.

CLICK! She bought the cows a car.

CLICK! She went again.
And booked the bull a holiday
Away in sunny Spain.

CLICK!
She bought the
horse a cart.

CLICK! She bought a boat.
The other chickens sailed away,
Amazed that they could float.

The little chick was all alone,
Cheepy, chirpy – CLICK!
"I'll find a friend online," she cheeped
"That will do the trick."

She bought herself a camera
Chirpy, chirpy – CLICK!
She preened her tiny feathers
And she posed and took her pic.

She put her photograph online
She gave her name and age.
CLICK! Another chick appeared
Upon the friendship page.

CLICK! They started chatting.
Chick had found the perfect chum
And off she went to meet her
Without telling Dad or Mum.

She went into the Wily Wood. And waited by a tree.
"I found a friend online!" she cheeped.

The fox said, "That was me!"